MW00909604

21st Century Skills Library

COOL SCIENCE CAREERS

VOLCANOLOGIST

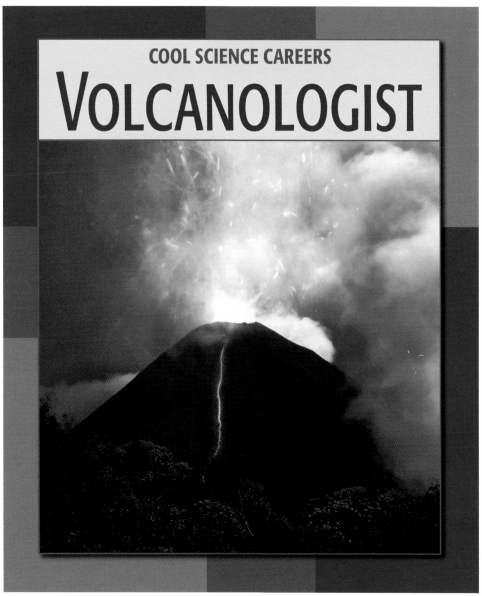

Kathleen Manatt

Cherry Lake Publishing
Ann Arbor, Michigan

Cherry Lake
12/1/07
18.95

Published in the United States of America by Cherry Lake Publishing
Ann Arbor, MI
www.cherrylakepublishing.com

Photo Credits: Page 7, © Roger Ressmeyer/CORBIS; Page 9, © Rob Howard/CORBIS;
Page 11, © Roger Ressmeyer/CORBIS; Page 18, Courtesy of USGS; USAF photo by
R. Batalon; Page 20, Photo Courtesy of USGS, Page 22, Photo Courtesy of USGS;
Page 24, Courtesy of USGS; Photo by J.D. Griggs

Library of Congress Cataloging-in-Publication Data
Manatt, Kathleen G.
  Volcanologist / by Kathleen Manatt.
    p. cm.—(Cool science careers)
  ISBN-13: 978-1-60279-050-6 (hardcover)   978-1-60279-085-8 (pbk.)
  ISBN-10: 1-60279-050-7 (hardcover)   1-60279-085-X (pbk.)
  1. Volcanologists—Juvenile literature. 2. Volcanoes—Vocational guidance—Juvenile literature.
I. Title. II. Series.
  QE521.3.M265 2008
  551.023—dc22   2007005663

Cherry Lake Publishing would like to acknowledge the work of
The Partnership for 21st Century Skills.
Please visit www.21stcenturyskills.org for more information.

TABLE of CONTENTS

CHAPTER ONE

A DEADLY DAY IN POMPEII

*Some of Pompeii has now been excavated, but
it still sits at the foot of deadly Vesuvius.*

The day of August 24, 79 A.D., was a hot but cloudy one in Pompeii. The Roman resort town was still recovering from an **earthquake** 15 years before. However, many of the luxurious homes had been rebuilt, and the town was full of shops, restaurants, and theaters.

Nearby Mt. Vesuvius was sending smoke up into the sky, and the ground often shook. Nobody paid much attention until things changed—drastically—in the afternoon.

The cloud from Mt. Vesuvius grew much darker and rose high into the sky. Tons of rocks fell on Pompeii, and ash filled the air. People could hardly

Over the centuries, Pompeii was forgotten. It was accidentally discovered in 1748 and is now a time capsule of life more than 1,900 years ago. What can we learn from such discoveries?

Learning & Innovation Skills

What are the ways that volcanoes are dangerous? You might revisit your list after reading the rest of this book.

see where they were going. They choked on the ash and died. One of them was a scientist named Pliny. He had rowed out into the bay to observe events and died from inhaling ash. Pompeii was buried under dozens of feet (meters) of ash and rock. No one ever lived there again.

CHAPTER TWO

BEING A VOLCANOLOGIST

*To do their jobs, volcanologists must go where the volcanoes are,
which is often into the heart of danger.*

When Pompeii was destroyed, scientists like Pliny had only a very

hazy understanding of **volcanoes**. They didn't know what caused volcanic

eruptions. Nor did they know how to recognize the signs that an

eruption might be near.

Today some scientists spend their entire careers studying volcanoes. They are called **volcanologists**. The volcanoes they study can be very smelly, very hot, and very dangerous. Many volcanologists believe they have the best jobs in the world, though.

What kinds of people want to become volcanologists? They must like being outside a lot. They often spend several months a year living in tents. They are not worried about being away from home for many months at a time. They are physically fit. They like adventure, and they like to solve mysteries. They also like that they can save lives by

figuring out when a volcano is

about to explode and warning

people to move far away.

Volcanologists collect **data**

about the volcanoes they study.

They set up machines called

seismometers inside and around

volcanoes that record small

movements in the ground. The

machine must be very securely set

in the ground so the recordings

will be accurate. By analyzing

Volcanologists must provide regular maintenance for the seismometers and other equipment they set up near volcanoes.

these recordings, the volcanologists may be able to show that a volcano is becoming more active.

Volcanologists film and photograph volcanoes to detect any bulges that might be forming in the top or sides. These bulges can be warnings of great danger to occur soon. Sometimes, the volcanologists use just plain cameras. Other times they use laser beams.

These are very precise beams of light that can determine if the volcano is inflating. If it is bulging, then the volcanologists know that activity is taking place below the surface and that there may be an eruption soon.

Volcanologists collect samples of **magma** and analyze it. By studying the magma, they can determine the precise makeup of the new rock when it cools. They can determine how much gas the magma contains. This is a clue to how violent the next eruption will be. If the gas can escape easily, a lot of ash may shoot into the air. If not, the magma may flow out in red-hot streams.

Volcanologists often wear special clothing to protect them from the intense heat of magma flows.

21st Century Content

The area around the Pacific Ocean is called the Ring of Fire. What does this name say about the volcanoes in the area? Nations that are part of the Ring of Fire include Canada, the United States, Peru, Mexico, Japan, New Zealand, and the Philippines, among others.

Volcanologists also study volcanoes that have recently erupted, which can help predict future events. They study new rock formations. They take samples from inside the **crater** if possible. They carefully study the shape and size of the mountain that remains. Obviously, this information can be of great help to people who live nearby. It can also generally increase our knowledge about volcanoes worldwide.

12

CHAPTER THREE

HOW VOLCANOES WORK

Mt. Etna is the largest active volcano in Europe, and its documented eruptions go back more than 2,000 years.

Volcanoes are very complicated, and each one is different. Right now, there are about 600 "active" volcanoes around the world. Many are near the Pacific Ocean. More than half of all volcanoes in the world are located

there. Active volcanoes might erupt some time in the future. Other volcanoes are called "extinct." These are believed to have no possibility of future eruption.

Volcanoes form where there is a tear in the earth's crust. The tear or vent allows the magma, hot gases, and hot rocks to erupt through the crust. Sometimes the magma flows out fairly peacefully. This is happening now in Hawaii.

Another kind of volcano forms when the magma is prevented from flowing smoothly. Pressure builds up, and eventually the volcano explodes. However, this process can take a very, very long time. "Eventually" may mean many thousands of years.

The Karymsky volcano is in far western Russia and has erupted more than 50 times since 2000. Fortunately, few people live nearby.

Many volcanoes form some type of mountain from the tons and tons

and tons of ash, lava, rocks, and cinders that have blown out of the ground.

However, it is sometimes hard to see the mountain. Take Crater Lake in

Oregon for example. It's a volcano, but it looks more like a lake today.

A huge eruption about 7,000 years ago caused the top of the volcano to

collapse. Melted snow has formed a deep lake in the collapsed top.

CHAPTER FOUR

WHEN THINGS BLEW UP

*Some of the area around Krakatau was so devastated
by the 1883 eruption that people never returned,
and it is now part of a national park.*

Krakatau was a small island in the South Pacific Ocean. Recorded

volcanic eruptions go back as far as the year 416, but 1883 was the year

of the really big one. In the years just before 1883, Krakatau had several

big earthquakes. Some of them were felt almost 2,000 miles (3,218 km) away in Australia. Then some relatively big volcanic explosions began on June 19, 1883. After that, things only got worse.

On August 27, a huge explosion occurred at 5:30 A.M., and three more followed. The final explosion was at 10:02 A.M. It was the biggest and loudest of all. It was heard almost 3,000 miles (4,827 km) away. It was the loudest noise in recorded history. The island was blown apart, and more than 36,000 people died. The eruption also caused **tsunamis** as far away as the English Channel.

Today the same volcano is rebuilding. People there call it Anak Krakatau, which means "child of Krakatau."

Learning & Innovation Skills

The final explosion of Krakatau was so loud that if it had occurred in New York City, people in Los Angeles would have been able to hear it. About how far can people be from you for you to still hear them? What does this tell you about how loud the sound was?

Volcanologists' warnings made the evacuation from near Mt. Pinatubo the most successful in history.

Mt. Pinatubo

Mt. Pinatubo was a sleeping giant. This volcano on Luzon, the largest

and most heavily populated island in the Philippines, had not erupted

for 400 years. Things changed in 1991, though. Mt. Pinatubo started

rumbling, and volcanologists took note. More than a million people

lived near the volcano. Thanks to the scientists'
warnings, tens of thousands of people moved out
of harm's way.

On June 15, 1991, Mt. Pinatubo blew up. A
giant ash cloud rose more than 20 miles (32.2 km)
in the air. The **debris** in the air caused temperatures
worldwide to dip for several years. Whole towns
were destroyed, and more than a foot (0.3 meter)
of ash fell.

However, warnings by volcanologists had saved
thousands of lives. The death toll was less than 800.
Most of those deaths were caused by buildings that
collapsed under the weight of the ash.

Many people have moved back to the Mt. Pinatubo area. Do you think this is a responsible thing to do? Hint: What will the effects be when the volcano blows again?

CHAPTER FIVE

THREE VOLCANOES IN THE UNITED STATES

Today, volcanologists constantly monitor Mt. St. Helens in Washington state using video cameras and other tools.

The United States has many active volcanoes. Most are in Alaska,

Hawaii, and the western third of the continental United States. The United

States Geological Survey (USGS) has volcano observatories in each place.

Volcanologists staff the observatories and look for signs of volcanic activity. When activity is found, the volcanologists warn nearby people.

Mt. St. Helens

People had seen this Washington state volcano erupt before, but no one had ever seen anything like what happened in 1980. Beginning in the early spring, the area was shaken by more than 10,000 little earthquakes. There were hundreds of small steam explosions from the top of the volcano, too. Even more ominous, the north side of the volcano began to bulge. It finally stretched outward more than 260 feet (79.3 meters).

21st Century Content

Imagine that you owned land near Mt. St. Helens and you were considering building a business there. What economic considerations do you have to take into account because of the volcano?

Government volcanologist David Johnston was the only person to correctly predict the nature of the Mt. St. Helens eruption.

At 8:32 A.M. on May 18, 1980, a major earthquake shook the mountain.

Within seconds, the bulging side became the largest landslide in recorded

history. It released a 300-degree blast of gas, steam, and rocks, moving

faster than a jet plane. The blast melted tons of snow and ice and sent a huge river of mud, water, and rock racing through the valley below. It covered the valley with debris up to 640 feet (195 meters) deep.

Mt. St. Helens is in an area that had little population in 1980. Still, 57 died in the eruption. Among the victims was volcanologist David A. Johnston, who was working nearby. Moments before the hot ash cloud hit him, Johnston radioed to faraway coworkers, saying "Vancouver! Vancouver! This is it!" His body was never found.

The Hawaiian Volcanoes

The state of Hawaii is made up of a group of islands that were all formed by volcanoes. Two of

There are active volcanoes on Antarctica, the southern tip of South America, and other isolated places. How is the eruption of a volcano there different than Mt. St. Helens?

Scientists estimate that Mauna Loa has a volume of 9,600 cubic miles (40,000 cubic km), making it the largest volcano on Earth.

these volcanoes, Mauna Loa and Kilauea, are located quite close to each

other on the same island. Mauna Loa is also among the world's most active

volcanoes. It has erupted more than 30 times since 1840. Volcanologists are

sure it will erupt again.

Kilauea is smaller than Mauna Loa, but it has a distinction that Mauna Loa can't beat. Kilauea has been erupting continuously since 1983! The relatively safe eruptions of Mauna Loa and Kilauea have made it possible for volcanologists to study them quite closely. The USGS has had an observatory there since 1912, and Hawaii Volcanoes National Park was created in 1916. Many tourists also come to see the volcanoes and their **lava** flows.

Here's what park rangers recommend to visitors.

- Wear closed-toe shoes to protect your feet and gardening gloves to protect your hands in case you fall on the hot, razor-sharp ground.

Studying lava samples helps volcanologists understand what is happening below ground with a specific volcano, but collecting the samples is an extremely dangerous thing to do. Preparing very carefully and having strong nerves are both requirements for success.

*Signs at Hawaii Volcanoes National Park clearly warn
tourists of the deadly dangers nearby.*

- Take lots of water to drink. The place can be like a sauna!

- Stay away from the deadly cloud of hydrochloric acid where lava

  flows into the ocean.

- ALWAYS stay in the areas marked as safe. Otherwise, you may fall

  through some thin lava crust and die.

CHAPTER SIX

LOOKING INTO THE FUTURE

*Warnings from government volcanologists about the sleeping
Mt. Rainier have led nearby people to hold regular evacuation drills.*

21st Century Content

Active volcanoes also threaten Tokyo, Japan, and Mexico City, Mexico. Tokyo is close to Mt. Fuji, where there have been 17 eruptions in recorded history. The last one was about 300 years ago. Today more than 12 million people live nearby. Mexico City is close to Popocatepetl, which has had 15 major eruptions in the last 500 years, although there has been some activity there every year since 2000. About 20 million people live nearby.

Millions of people live near active volcanoes.

One is Mt. Rainier near Seattle, Washington, where 1.5 million people live. It erupted 160 years ago.

That's just the blink of an eye in volcano time. Not only could a major explosion send lava and ash clouds down into the city, Mt. Rainier is also covered with snow. The heat of an eruption would probably melt the snow and send it racing down on top of people.

Volcanologists carefully monitor all active volcanoes, but they especially track the ones near major cities. They also hold regular international conferences to share their knowledge. In the United States, USGS volcanologists and others study active American volcanoes continually. So even though a volcano can kill you, scientists today are watching to make sure that doesn't happen.

21st Century Content

In June 2006 an earthquake in Indonesia caused increased activity in Mt. Merapi, a volcano about 250 miles east of Jakarta, the capital city. Volcanologists as well as advanced teams of relief groups from the United States, Europe, and Asia prepared to go there if an eruption occurred.

GLOSSARY

crater (KREY-ter) bowl-shaped depression at the mouth of a volcano

data (DEY-tuh) factual information for analysis

debris (duh-BREE) scattered remains of something broken or destroyed

earthquake (URTH-kweyk) sudden movement of the Earth's surface, usually caused by the release of underground stress

lava (LAH-vuh) melted rock that reaches the Earth's surface

magma (MAG-muh) melted rock material under the Earth's crust

tsunamis (tsoo-NAH-meez) huge ocean waves that travel at high speeds (sometimes hitting land)

volcanoes (vol-KEY-nohz) places where magma pours out of the ground

volcanologists (vol-kuh-NOL-uh-jists) scientists who study volcanoes

FOR MORE INFORMATION

Books

Caplan, Jeremy. *Time for Kids: Volcanoes!*
New York: Harper Collins, 2006.

Cole, Joanna and Degen, Bruce. *Voyage to the Volcano*.
New York: Scholastic, Inc., 2003.

Lindop, Laurie. *Probing Volcanoes*.
Brookfield, CT: Twenty-First Century Books, 2003.

O'Brien-Palmer, Michelle. *How the Earth Works: 60 Fun Activities for Exploring Volcanoes, Fossils, Earthquakes, and More*.
Chicago: Chicago Review Press, 2002.

Thompson, Luke. *Natural Disasters: Volcanoes*.
New York: Children's Press, 2000.

Van Cleve, Janice. *Volcanoes: Mind-Boggling Experiments You Can Turn Into Science Fair Projects*.
New York: John Wiley and Sons, 1994.

Other Media

For an online game about volcanoes in the United States, go to
http://volcano.und.edu/vwdocs/kids/fun/ usa_matching/Matching.html

For information about every active volcano in the world, go to
http://volcano.und.edu/vwdocs/volc_images/sorted_by_country.html

For more information about how volcanoes work, go to
http://www.geology.sdsu.edu/how_volcanoes_work/Home.html

Understanding Volcanoes. DVD. Educational Video Network, 1987.

INDEX

ABOUT THE AUTHOR

Kathleen Manatt is a long-time writer, editor, and publisher of books for children. Many of her books have been about faraway places, which she likes to visit. She grew up in Illinois, Iowa, New Jersey, and California, and lived in Chicago for many years as an adult. She has climbed pyramids in Mexico, ridden elephants in Thailand, and toured the fjords of Norway. She has also visited Moscow, Lisbon, Paris, Geneva, London, Madrid, Edinburgh, and Barcelona. She now lives in Austin, Texas.